MOODY
MARGARET'S
School

MOODY
MARGARET'S
School

Francesca Simon
Illustrated by Tony Ross

Orion
Children's Books

Moody Margaret's School originally appeared in
Horrid Henry Robs the Bank first published in Great Britain in 2008
by Orion Children's Books
This edition first published in Great Britain in 2011
by Orion Children's Books
a division of the Orion Publishing Group Ltd
Orion House
5 Upper Saint Martin's Lane
London WC2H 9EA
An Hachette UK Company

1 3 5 7 9 10 8 6 4 2

A catalogue record for this book is available from the British Library.

ISBN 978 1 4440 0108 2

Printed and bound in China

www.orionbooks.co.uk
www.horridhenry.co.uk

To Sue Michniewicz,
for all her lovely work on Horrid Henry

Look out for . . .

Don't Be Horrid, Henry!
Horrid Henry's Birthday Party
Horrid Henry's Holiday
Horrid Henry's Underpants
Horrid Henry Gets Rich Quick
Horrid Henry and the Football Fiend
Horrid Henry's Nits
Horrid Henry and Moody Margaret
Horrid Henry's Thank You Letter
Horrid Henry Reads A Book
Horrid Henry's Car Journey

There are many more **Horrid Henry** books
available. For a complete list visit
www.horridhenry.co.uk
or
www.orionbooks.co.uk

Contents

Chapter 1

"Pay attention, Susan,"
shrieked Moody Margaret,
"or you'll go straight to the head."

"I *am* paying attention,"
said Sour Susan.

"This is boring,"
said Horrid Henry.
"I want to play pirates."

"Silence," said Moody Margaret,
whacking her ruler on the table.

"I want to be the teacher,"
said Susan.

"No," said Margaret.

"*I'll* be the teacher," said Horrid
Henry. He'd send the class straight
out for playtime, and tell them
to run for their lives.

"Are you out of your mind?"
snapped Margaret.

"Can I be the teacher?"
asked Perfect Peter.

"NO!" shouted Margaret,
Susan, and Henry.

"Why can't I be the head?"
said Susan sourly.

"Because," said Margaret.

"'Cause why?" said Susan.

"'Cause *I'm* the head."

"But you're the head *and* the teacher," said Susan. "It's not fair."

"It is too fair, 'cause you'd make a terrible head," said Margaret.

"Wouldn't!"

"Would!"

"I think we should take turns being head," said Susan.

"That," said Margaret, "is the
dumbest idea I've ever heard.
Do you see Mrs Oddbod taking *turns*
being head? I don't think so."

Margaret's class grumbled
mutinously on the carpet inside
the Secret Club tent.

Chapter 2

"Class, I will now take
the register," intoned Margaret.

"Susan?"

Here.

"Peter?"

Here.

"Henry?"

"In the toilet."

Margaret scowled.
"We'll try that again. Henry?"

"Flushed away."

"Last chance,"
said Margaret severely. "Henry?"

"Dead."

Margaret made a big cross in
her register.
"I will deal with you later."

"No one made *you* the big boss,"
muttered Horrid Henry.

"It's *my* house and we'll play what
I want," said Moody Margaret.
"And I want to play school."

Horrid Henry scowled.

Whenever Margaret came to
his house she was the guest and
he had to play what *she* wanted.
But whenever Henry went to
her house Margaret was the boss
'cause it was *her* house.

Ugggh.

Why oh why did he have to live
next door to Moody Margaret?

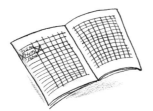

Chapter 3

Mum had important work to do,
and needed total peace and quiet,
so Henry and Peter had been
dumped at Margaret's.

Henry had begged to go
to Ralph's, but Ralph was visiting
his grandparents.

Now he was trapped all day with
a horrible, moody old grouch.

Wasn't it bad enough being with Miss Battle-Axe all week without having to spend his whole precious Saturday stuck at Margaret's? And, even worse, playing school?

"Come on, let's play pirates,"
said Henry.
"I'm Captain Hook.
Peter, walk the plank!"

"No," said Margaret.
"I don't want to."

"But I'm the guest,"
protested Henry.

"So?" said Margaret.
"This is *my* house and
we play by *my* rules."

"Yeah, Henry," said Sour Susan.

"And I love playing school,"
said Perfect Peter.
"It's such fun doing sums."

Grrr.

If only Henry could just go home.

"I want a good report,"
Mum had said, "or you won't be
going to Dave's bowling party
tonight. It's very kind of Margaret
and her mum to have you boys
over to play."

"But I don't want to go to Margaret's!" howled Henry. "I want to stay home and watch TV!"

"N–O spells no,"

said Mum, and sent him kicking and screaming next door. "You can come home at five o'clock to get ready for Dave's party and not a minute before."

Horrid Henry gazed longingly
over the wall.

His house looked so inviting.
There was his bedroom window,
twinkling at him.

And his lonesome telly, stuck all by itself in the sitting room, just begging him to come over and switch it on.

And all his wonderful toys, just waiting to be played with.

Funny, thought Horrid Henry, his toys seemed so boring when he was in his room. But now that he was trapped at Margaret's, there was so much he longed to do at home.

Wait.

He could hide out in his fort until five. Yes!
Then he'd stroll into his house as if he'd been at Margaret's all day.

But then Margaret's mum would
be sure to call his mum to say that
Henry had vanished and Henry
would get into trouble.

Big, big
trouble.
Big, big,
banned from
Dave's party trouble.

Or, he'd pretend to be sick.
Margaret's mum was such an
old fusspot she'd be sure to send
him home immediately.

Yippee.

He was a genius. This would be easy.

A few loud coughs, a few dramatic
clutches at his stomach, a dash to the
loo, and he'd be sent straight home
and …

Oops. He'd be put to bed.

No party.

No pizza.

No bowling.

And what was the point of pretending to be sick at the *weekend*? He was trapped.

Chapter 4

Moody Margaret whacked her ruler on the table.

"I want everyone to write
a story," said Margaret.

Write a story!
Boy would Horrid Henry write
a story. He seized a piece of paper
and a pencil and scribbled away.

"Who'd like to read their story to the class?" said Margaret.

"I will," said Henry.

Once upon a time there was a moody old grouch named Margaret.

Margaret had been born a frog but an ugly wizard cursed the frog and turned it into Margaret.

"That's enough, Henry,"
snapped Margaret.

Henry ignored her.

"Ribbet ribbet,"
said Margaret Frog.
"Ribbet ribbet ribbet."
Everyone in the kingdom
tried to get rid of this
horrible croaking moody
monster. But she smelled
so awful that no one could
get near her.

And then one day a hero
named Heroic Henry came,
and he held his nose, grabbed
the Margaret Monster and
hurled her into outer space
where she exploded and was
never seen again.

THE END

Susan giggled.

Margaret glared.

"Fail," said Margaret.

"Why?" said Horrid Henry innocently.

"'Cause," said Margaret. "I'm the teacher and I say it was boring."

"Did you think my story was boring, Peter?" demanded Henry.

Peter looked nervous.

"Did you?" said Margaret.

"Well, uhm, uhmm, I think mine is better," said Peter.

Once upon a time there was a tea towel named Terry. He was a very sad tea towel because he didn't have any dishes to dry. One day he found a lot of wet dishes. Swish swish swish, they were dry in no time. "Yippee," said Terry the Tea Towel, "I wonder when —"

"Boring!" shouted Horrid Henry.

"Excellent, Peter,"
said Moody Margaret.
"*Much* better than Henry's."

Susan read out a story about her cat.

My cat Kitty Kat is a big fat cat.

She says meow.

One day Kitty Kat met a dog.

Meow, said Kitty Kat.

Woof woof, said the dog.

Kitty Kat ran away.

So did the dog.

The end.

"OK, class, here are your marks," said Margaret. "Peter came first."

"Yay!" said Perfect Peter.

"*What?*" said Susan. "My story was way better than his."

"Susan came second,
Henry came ninth."

"How can I be ninth if there are only three people in the class?" demanded Horrid Henry.

"'Cause that's how bad your story was," said Margaret. "Now, I've done some worksheets for you. No talking or there'll be no break."

"Goody," said Perfect Peter.
"I love worksheets. Are there lots
of hard spelling words to learn?

Chapter 5

Horrid Henry had had enough.
It was time to turn into
Heroic Henry and destroy this
horrible hag.

Henry crumpled up his worksheet
and stood up.
"I've just been pretending to
be a student," shouted Henry.
"In fact, I'm a school inspector.
And I'm shutting your school down.
It's a disgrace."

Margaret gasped.

"You're a moody old grouch
and a terrible teacher,"
said the inspector.

"I am not," said Margaret.

"She is not," said Susan.

"Silence when the inspector
is speaking! You're the worst teacher
I've ever seen. Imagine marking
a stupid story about a tea towel
higher than a fantastic tale about
a wicked wizard."

"I'm the head," said Margaret.
"You can't boss me around."

"I'm the inspector," said Henry.
"I can boss *everyone* around."

"Wrong, Henry," said Margaret,
"because I'm the *chief* school
inspector, and I'm inspecting *you*."

"Oh no you're not,"

said Henry.

"Oh yes I am,"

said Margaret.

"An inspector can't be a head
and a teacher, so there,"
said Henry.

"Oh yes I can,"

said Margaret.

"No you can't, 'cause I'm king and I send you to the Tower!" shrieked King Henry the Horrible.

"I'm the empress!" screamed Margaret. "Go to jail."

"I'm king of the universe,
and I send you to the snakepit,"
shrieked Henry.

"I'm queen of the universe and I'm
going to chop off your head!"

"Not if I chop off yours first!"
shrieked the king, yanking
on the queen's hair.

The queen screamed
and kicked the king.

The king screamed
and kicked the queen.

"MUM!" screamed Margaret.

Chapter 6

Margaret's mother rushed into
the Secret Club tent.

"What's wrong with my little snugglechops?" said Margaret's mum.

"Henry's not playing my game," said Margaret. "And he kicked me."

"She kicked me first," said Henry.

"If you children can't play nicely I'll have to send you all home," said Margaret's mother severely.

"No!" said Peter.

Send him ... home.

Yes!

Henry would make Margaret scream
until the walls fell down.
He would tell Margaret's mum
her house smelled of poo.
He could ... he would ...

But if Henry was sent home for
being horrid, Mum and Dad would
be furious. There'd be no pizza and
bowling party for sure.

Unless … unless … It was risky.
It was dangerous. It could go
horribly, horribly wrong.
But desperate times call for
desperate measures.

"Need a drink," said Henry,
and ran out of the tent before
Margaret could stop him.

Henry went into the kitchen
to find Margaret's mum.

"I'm worried about Margaret, I think she's getting sick," said Henry.

"My little Maggie-muffin?" gasped Margaret's mum.

"She's being very strange," said Henry sadly. "She said she's the queen of the world and she would cut off my head."

"Margaret would *never* say such
a thing," said her mum. "She always
plays beautifully. I've never seen
a child so good at sharing."

Horrid Henry nodded.
"I know. It must be 'cause she's sick.
Maybe she caught something
from Peter."

"Has Peter been ill?" said Margaret's mum. She looked pale.

"Oh yeah," lied Henry. "He's been throwing up, and – and – well, it's been awful. But I'm sure he's not *very* contagious."

"Throwing up?"
said Margaret's mum weakly.

"And diarrhoea," said Henry.
"Loads and loads."

Margaret's mother looked ashen.
"Diarrhoea?"

"But he's much better now," said
Henry. "He's only run to the loo
five times since we've been here."

Margaret's mother looked faint.
"My little Margaret is so delicate …
I can't risk …" she gasped. "I think
you and Peter had better go home
straight away. Margaret! Margaret!
Come in at once," she shouted.

Horrid Henry did not wait to be told twice. School was out!

Ahhhh, thought Horrid Henry
happily, reaching for the TV clicker,
this was the life.

Margaret had been sent to bed.
He and Peter had been sent home.

There was enough time to watch
Marvin the Maniac and *Terminator
Gladiator* before Dave's party.

"I can't help it that Margaret
wasn't feeling well, Mum,"
said Horrid Henry.
"I just hope I haven't caught
anything from *her*."

Honestly.
Mum was so selfish.

HORRID HENRY BOOKS

Horrid Henry
Horrid Henry and the Secret Club
Horrid Henry Tricks the Tooth Fairy
Horrid Henry's Nits
Horrid Henry Gets Rich Quick
Horrid Henry's Haunted House
Horrid Henry and the Mummy's Curse
Horrid Henry's Revenge
Horrid Henry and the Bogey Babysitter
Horrid Henry's Stinkbomb
Horrid Henry's Underpants
Horrid Henry Meets the Queen
Horrid Henry and the Mega-Mean Time Machine
Horrid Henry and the Football Fiend
Horrid Henry's Christmas Cracker
Horrid Henry and the Abominable Snowman
Horrid Henry Robs the Bank
Horrid Henry Wakes the Dead
Horrid Henry Rocks

Colour books
Horrid Henry's Big Bad Book
Horrid Henry's Wicked Ways
Horrid Henry's Evil Enemies
Horrid Henry Rules the World
Horrid Henry's House of Horrors
Horrid Henry's Dreadful Deeds
Horrid Henry Shows Who's Boss

Joke Books

Horrid Henry's Joke Book
Horrid Henry's Jolly Joke Book
Horrid Henry's Mighty Joke Book
Horrid Henry's Hilariously Horrid Joke Book
Horrid Henry's Purple Hand Gang Joke Book

Early Readers

Don't be Horrid, Henry
Horrid Henry's Birthday Party
Horrid Henry's Holiday
Horrid Henry's Underpants
Horrid Henry Gets Rich Quick
Horrid Henry and the Football Fiend
Horrid Henry's Nits
Horrid Henry and Moody Margaret
Horrid Henry's Thank You Letter
Horrid Henry Reads A Book
Horrid Henry's Car Journey

Horrid Henry is also available on CD and as a digital download, all read by Miranda Richardson.